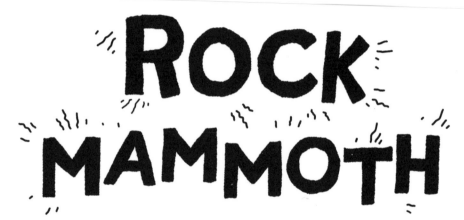

ROCK MAMMOTH

Eveline Payette
Guillaume Perreault

TRANSLATED BY Karen Simon

ORCA BOOK PUBLISHERS

To Juliette, Madeleine, and Louis, for the mammoth-size love.
To Michel, for the rock.
—E.P.

To my father, who handed down to me his curiosity
and desire to always learn more.
—G.P.

Text copyright © Eveline Payette 2020
Illustrations copyright © Guillaume Perreault 2020
Translation copyright © Karen Simon 2020
Originally published in French in 2017 by Les éditions la courte échelle under the title *Mammouth Rock*

Cataloguing in Publication information available from Library and Archives Canada
Issued in print and electronic formats.
ISBN 9781459824263 (softcover) | ISBN 9781459824270 (PDF) | ISBN 9781459824287 (EPUB)

Library of Congress Control Number: 2019947381
Simultaneously published in Canada and the United States in 2020

Summary: Louis has to do a presentation on his pet mammoth in this elementary illustrated novel.

Orca Book Publishers is committed to reducing the consumption of nonrenewable resources in the making of our books. We make every effort to use materials that support a sustainable future.

Orca Book Publishers gratefully acknowledges the support for its publishing programs provided by the following agencies: the Government of Canada, the Canada Council for the Arts and the Province of British Columbia through the BC Arts Council and the Book Publishing Tax Credit.

We acknowledge the financial support of the Government of Canada through the National Translation Program for Book Publishing, an initiative of the *Roadmap for Canada's Official Languages 2013–2018: Education, Immigration, Communities*, for our translation activities.

Cover and interior artwork by Guillaume Perreault
Translated by Karen Simon

ORCA BOOK PUBLISHERS
orcabook.com

Printed and bound in China.

23 22 21 20 • 4 3 2 1

Mammoths lived millions of years ago, in prehistoric times. These enormous mammals belonged to the family Elephantidae. They were distant cousins of the elephants we know today. They first appeared in Africa but then spread throughout the world.

Researchers discovered the first traces of *Mammuthus* in the bitter cold of Siberia.

The famous Icelandic researcher Voïvoden Mamouten was there. He's my hero. Did you notice his last name? These spectacular beasts are called mammoths in his honor.

It's said that Voïvoden Mamouten was very shy. He was pretty much a recluse. He was also surprisingly hairy. Nearly as hairy as a mammoth. Throughout his life, his friends and scientific colleagues made fun of him for being so shy and so hairy.

The true and not funny story of Voïvoden Mamouten:

1. Baby Mamouten looks so much like a mammoth that he scares his parents.

2. Little Mamouten is teased in grade school because of his long hair.

3. The teenage Mamouten has no success in romance.

4. At university everyone makes fun of the strange, hairy student.

5. Mamouten is even the laughingstock of his scientific colleagues.

But inside little Voïvoden's big, hairy head was an imposing brain. His scientific mind was phenomenal.

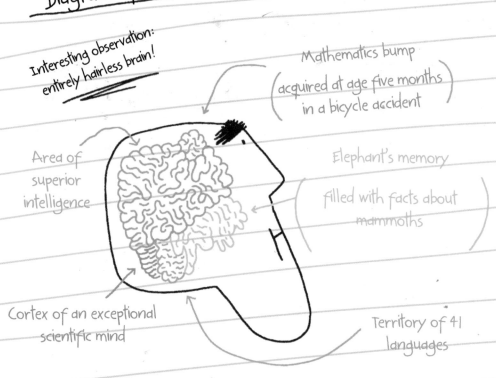

Diagram of Voïvoden Mamouten's brain

Interesting observation: entirely hairless brain!

Mathematics bump
(acquired at age five months in a bicycle accident)

Area of superior intelligence

Elephant's memory

filled with facts about mammoths

Cortex of an exceptional scientific mind

Territory of 41 languages

Researchers had discovered eleven species of *Mammuthus* in Siberia. But then the great Voïvoden discovered a twelfth—*Mammuthus rockus*. This is my favorite species. It's smart and it's cool. My report is on this rock mammoth.

Mammuthus rockus has a long, woolly coat and the same large tusks as his elephant cousins. However, he is smaller and surprisingly flexible. He is also able to emit impressive shouts.

In fact, *Mammuthus rockus* is like the rock 'n' roll singers of the 1970s who my father imitates when he thinks no one is looking. Dad plays solos on his tennis racket and even pretends to plug it into a radiator as if it were an amp. When my father plays his tennis-racket guitar, my mother sings backup on her hairbrush mic. She sings at the top of her lungs. Her voice sounds like a pterodactyl whose wing has been caught in a tyrannosaurus's trap. I must admit, it's pretty embarrassing.

Specimen comparison

↙ Mammuthus rockus

- Long, woolly coat
- Large tusks
- Small size, surprisingly flexible
- Rallying cries ("Good evening, Siberia!")

Louis's dad

- Absence of woolly coat on head
- No tusks
- Big size, not flexible
- Incomprehensible cries
  ("Dazednconfusedoooooohbaby!")

Louis's mom

- Thick and tangled woolly coat
- Can defend herself
- Medium size, medium flexibility
- Unbearable cries (excellent defense
  mechanism against predators)

Conclusion:
Louis's parents = not rock mammoths

Rock mammoths were awesome!

They're often in the drawings prehistoric people chalked on the walls of their caves.

See the people running after the mammoths, carrying long, pointy pens? Researchers think they are trying to get mammoth autographs.

Some of the drawings lead us to believe that rock mammoths wrote a lot of popular songs. The Cro-Magnon people in the cave drawings often have their mouths wide open, their eyes closed and their fists in the air. It's thought that they got together to sing the tunes of their mammoth rock'n'roll favorites.

Voïvoden Mamouten even discovered drawings of prehistoric people fainting as these colossal celebrities passed by.

One day all the rock mammoths disappeared. No one knows where they went or why they vanished. They left no trace.

It's a mystery.

A mystery is when you don't know the answer to an important question.

Like when my mother can't find a single cookie in the bag she just bought. 'Who ate all the cookies?' she asks.

'Not me!' everyone answers.

Then she says, 'It's a mystery. It's probably the cookie ghost who lives in our attic.'

Definition of mystery

Mystery = not knowing the answer
to an important question

Examples of
mysteries:

??
?
?

(A) How were the
pyramids built?

(B) How could Beethoven compose
symphonies if he was deaf?

(C) Why, when I put two socks in the wash, does
only one come out?

(D) Are we alone in the universe? If so, why do I always have
to turn down the TV?

Louis, you're digressing.
Please get back to
your report.

Researchers proposed a hypothesis about the disappearance of rock mammoths.

A hypothesis is a possible solution to a mystery.

It's important not to confuse the word *hypothesis* with *prosthesis*.

Definition of hypothesis

Hypothesis = idea

✱ NOT TO BE CONFUSED WITH:

Dental prosthesis = denture

Peloponnesus = region in Greece

Aunt Janice = moustached relative we see at Christmas who pinches our cheeks and says we've grown and also makes amazing maple fudge

Mayonnaise = sandwich condiment

In my family we talk a lot about a certain prosthesis when Grandma comes to visit.

Grandma's hard of hearing, so Dad has to shout:

MOM, YOU FORGOT YOUR DENTURES IN THE GLASS OF WATER ON THE COUNTER! I ALMOST SWALLOWED THEM WHEN I TOOK A SIP!

I must admit, their shouting is pretty embarrassing.

LOU-IS!!!!! Get back to your report.

Right. Back to the rock mammoth.

Here are some of the hypotheses put forward by Mamouten and his colleagues about why the mammoths disappeared.

Some hypotheses regarding the disappearance of rock mammoths

Big earthquake

Volcanic eruption

Lice epidemic—all rock
mammoths infested

Super-duper nasty
bacteria

Violent storm

Sudden global
warming

Meteorite

Famine caused by a significant
shortage of cookies, which were
probably eaten by prehistoric ghosts

Not one of the researchers thought of *my* hypothesis—a mega game of hide-and-seek that went wrong.

You see, rock mammoths were very good at hiding and camouflaging themselves. We know this thanks to fossils discovered by Mamouten and his team. Rock mammoths often had to escape delirious fans running after them with giant pointy pens.

My hypothesis is that the mammoths were exhausted by life as Elephantidae stars. So they hid. Really well. So well that they were never found.

That's impossible. Mammoths are too big to hide!

Hypothetical hiding methods of the rock mammoth

Camouflaged amid rocks

Stretched out near a fire like a bearskin

Behind an Ursus spelaeus (cave bear to their friends)

Flattened against a cave wall

I know what you're thinking. You hate those fans with the pointy pens who forced rock mammoths into hiding.

Well, personally, I can understand *Mammuthus rockus fanaticus*, even the ones who tried to trap rock mammoths. It would be great to have a rock mammoth. They'd be cool friends, and they'd also be very handy.

Some household uses for a rock mammoth

- Comfortable winter blanket
- Fashion accessory
- Attractive camouflage for going incognito
- Ultra-absorbent, anti-spill sponge
- Luxurious chair
- Towel rack

- Giant toothpick with surgical precision
- Ideal knitting accessory
- Ecological carwash
- Anti-bullying tool
- Excellent closet-monster repellent
- Full-sized, cuddly animal friend

And, most especially, the perfect friend for hide-and-seek!

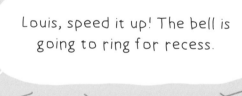

Louis, speed it up! The bell is going to ring for recess.

I'm almost through. I'm coming to the most fascinating part of my report.

My discovery!

To test my hypothesis, I read everything I could about mammoths. I took out every library book that my tyrannosaur-green backpack could hold without my bike falling over. The librarian and I ran several tests.

"Loading books about mammoths on a bike" tests with the librarian

Test 1

Adding the <u>Illustrated Encyclopedia of All Dinosaurs from the Big Bang to Today.</u>

AAAAAAAAAH!!!

Test 2

Removing the <u>Complete Bible of Mammoth Enthusiasts.</u>

AAAAAAH!
Help!

I read all day Saturday, from dawn until late at night!
I didn't leave my bed. Didn't eat. Didn't drink. I read
EVERYTHING!

My parents worried about me being in bed all day.
They visited every so often to make sure I was still
breathing.

Selected bibliography

- Our Friends the Mammoths
- Training a House Mammoth
- Memoir of a Rock Mammoth: Fame to Fiasco
- Doctor, a Mammoth Stepped on My Foot
- Call Me Voivoden: Autobiography
- Rock'n'Mammoth!

The following morning I woke up
looking like a mammoth!

I took this as a sign. I stood in front of the mirror and told myself, "Louis, what if it's your destiny to become *the* great researcher chosen by science to walk in the steps of Mamouten and pursue his work by finally discovering the great rock-mammoth hideout?!! What if *you* search for it? That would certainly give you an A+ on your oral report. Everyone on your street, at school, in the whole city, knows that your neighborhood is full of hard-to-find hiding places!"

I was fired up. I made a list of important things I had to do. It was the kind of list the great master would have drawn up before an expedition.

Between mouthfuls of cereal, I told Mom and Dad my plans.

'M gonna mafter favmammoth dday!!

Mmmm...what?

'M GONNA MAFTER FAVMAMMOTH DDAY!!

Okay. That's fine, Louis.

THE DAILY

wow!

ARTS

YO

I really think some things are better said between mouthfuls of cereal.

I made a list of the best hiding places on my street. I also made four irresistible tomato-and-mayo sandwiches on white, my favorite.

Tomato-and-mayonnaise was also Voïvoden Mamouten's favorite kind of sandwich, so I deduced that it was the perfect bait for mammoths.

Recipe for a good tomato-and-mayonnaise sandwich
on white bread to lure a rock mammoth

White bread (not brown—too
healthy for a rock star)

Mayonnaise slathered on top
piece of white bread

Tomato slices

Basil leaves
(secret ingredient)

Mayonnaise slathered on
bottom piece of white bread

I'm getting hungry!

The bell is going to ring
for recess. You have to
stop now, Louis.

But I'm coming to my
discovery. It's the key
to my whole report!

I followed my plan to the letter. I looked in all the interesting hiding places in my neighborhood.

In our hedge.

Under the porch.

Behind the shed at Khalim's house.

Even in my big sister's mega-secret-don't-come-in-under-any-circumstances-or-you're-dead bedroom.

No mammoth in sight. How was that possible? Was my hypothesis wrong?

Why didn't you try the garden behind old Mrs. Crane's house?

I sat on the porch to gather my thoughts. My hypothesis appeared to be weak.

I was terribly disappointed.

I emptied my sandwich bag and breathed into it, just like my mother suggests I do when things don't go as planned. I ate a sandwich for courage—and also because it looked really good. Then I closed my eyes and thought very hard.

Suddenly—I swear on the head of a rock mammoth—a shiny, hairy form appeared before me. I recognized him right away. It was Voïvoden Mamouten! The real Voïvoden Mamouten! He had a message for me.

Louis, pretend you are a mammoth. What would a mammoth do? YOU ARE a mammoth, Louis. Think like a mammoth. Make me proud and find a rock mammoth, Louis.

Then Voïvoden Mamouten vanished as quickly as he had appeared.

Ooooo ooooh!

I understood that I had been chosen!
Mamouten had chosen me to succeed him!
My mother has always said that I'm special.

RRRRRRINNNNG!

Time for recess!

No! We want to hear what comes next!

I closed my eyes again and tried to concentrate. I imagined myself in the skin of a rock mammoth. Then all of a sudden my intuition kicked in.

Intuition is when you're inspired with a new idea to verify a hypothesis that might solve a mystery.

It's important not to confuse intuition with emotion, which is what my sister feels when she sees her favorite singer on TV. My sister is quite embarrassing.

I thought hard. Rock mammoths are at ease in the cold because of their long, woolly coats. According to my hypothesis, they're the ancestors of the singers of the 1970s, who gave huge concerts and filled giant halls and amphitheaters.

Cold + amphitheater = arena

I got it! They were hiding at the arena!

I rushed to the town arena. When I arrived a bunch of skaters were spinning on the ice. This wasn't exactly a place for mammoths. Therefore, it was an excellent hiding place.

I congratulated myself on my theory and my deduction skills. Mom thinks that loving yourself and having self-esteem are very important. I know because she has loads of books on the subject lying around the house.

Plan of the municipal arena

Ice rink
Rock mammoths like the
cold. Rock mammoth here?

Locker room
Rock mammoth here?

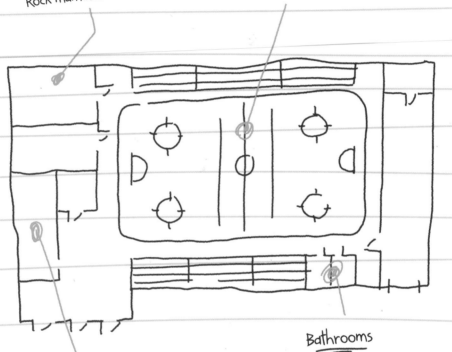

Snack bar
Rock mammoths probably love
hot dogs. Rock mammoth here?

Bathrooms
No rock mammoth here.
Yuck!

List of places explored

Under the bleachers
In the changing rooms
snack bar

I searched the entire arena. Nothing.

List of places explored
——————————————

Under the bleachers
In the changing rooms
At the snack bar

I sat down to think again. I took
another bite of my sandwich.
Thinking was giving me an
appetite.

The skaters went off to find
their parents. Hordes of hockey
players awaited their turn on
the ice. I was discouraged. I felt
unworthy of my hero. I was about
to abandon the whole thing. And
that's when the man came to
clean the ice, and I saw it...

Hidden under the Zamboni was
a mammoth!
A real, genuine mammoth!
All flattened out!

He was helping polish
the ice. What an incredible
hiding place!

Louis, that's just
nonsense.

Wow!

I was really impressed by the superior intelligence of this ancestral pachyderm.

At first glance, his size and flexibility seemed to confirm my impression that this beast belonged to the twelfth species. Had I found a rare specimen of *Mammuthus rockus*?

Comparison of the specimens

Mammuthus rockus	VS	Mammuthus arenus
Long, woolly coat	✗	Long, woolly coat
Large tusks	✗	Large tusks
Small size	✗	Small size
Astonishingly flexible	✗	Astonishingly flexible
Rallying cry: "Good evening, Siberia!"		Rallying cry not yet observed

On tippy-toes I snuck into the arena garage.

I waited for the Zamboni to finish its job.

I was as excited as a prehistoric flea. I felt like shouting like a rock singer. But I'm a serious researcher. I took three deep breaths and calmed down.

Carefully I put a tomato-mayo sandwich on white on the end of a hockey stick.

The woolly animal pulled itself out from under the machine to take a bite! (Honestly, who can resist a tomato-and-mayonnaise sandwich on white?) He devoured it in one bite and then licked each of his mayonnaise-smeared legs with pleasure. I *knew* that mammoths adored mayonnaise!

He looked at the last sandwich I was holding, then stared at me imploringly. (Honestly, I don't know anyone who could resist the imploring look of a rock mammoth.) I shared it with him, and we got to talking. The mammoth told me about his glory days as a star and about life as a recluse. I told him about my life as an eminent junior researcher.

We became friends. We don't see each other every day. He's a solitary fugitive, and he's afraid of being recognized. But my parents invite him to supper every Saturday evening. They love to put on amazing rock concerts for me and my sister!